★ TEACH YOURSELF ★

T·A·P DANCING

by Steven Caney with Peggy Spina

WORKMAN PUBLISHING, NEW YORK

Cover and book illustrations by Judith Sutton
(pages 16, 17, 19, 20, 21, 22, 23, 24, 25, 26, 27, 28, 29, 30, 31, 32, 33, 34, 35, 36, 37, 38, 52, 53, 54)

Back cover and additional book illustrations by Mike Quon Design Office

Photography credits:
Pages 6 – 8: Dance Collection,
New York Public Library at Lincoln Center.
Page 10: Jerry Ohlinger; Conrad Gloos.
Page 11: Jerry Ohlinger; Frank Driggs Collection.
Page 12: Frank Driggs Collection; Jerry Ohlinger.
Page 13: Jerry Ohlinger; Frank Driggs Collection.
Page 14: Jerry Ohlinger.
Pages 42 – 46: Jerry Ohlinger.
Page 48: Frank Driggs Collection.
Pages 49 – 64: Jerry Ohlinger.

Library of Congress Cataloging-in-Publication Data

Caney, Steven.
Teach yourself tap dancing / by Steven Caney.

p. cm.
Summary: Introduces the basic steps of tap dancing and how to create routines. Includes a set of taps and an audiocassette with lessons and songs.
ISBN 0-89480-428-6
1. Tap dancing — Juvenile literature.
(1.Tap dancing. 2. Dancing.) I Title.
GV1794.C35 1990
792.7 — dc20
89-40726
CIP
AC

Book design by Judy Doud Lewis

Workman Publishing Company, Inc.
708 Broadway
New York, New York 10003

Printed in the United States of America

First printing
10 9 8 7 6 5 4 3 2 1

CONTENTS

An American Invention..4

America's True Folk Dance..6

Stars of Tap Dancing..11

Start Off on the Right Foot..15

Lesson One: Stamp 21

Lesson Two: Ball Change 22

Lesson Three: Shuffle 24

Lesson Four: The Waltz Clog.......................................26

Lesson Five: More Things
    to Do With Your Feet 28

Lesson Six: Turns 37

Lesson Seven: Rhythms..39

Lesson Eight: Creating a Dance..................................43

Putting on a Show 47

More Tap! 56

AN AMERICAN INVENTION

Have you ever listened to music and tapped your foot in time to the beat? Have you ever drummed on a tabletop to make up a rhythm of your own? Then you're already on your way to learning tap dancing.

Tap dancing is like playing a musical instrument, but using your feet as the instrument! Metal taps attached to the bottoms of your shoes make the sounds, and the "music" is the rhythm of the shoes against a hard floor.

In tap dancing, what you hear is as important as what you see. In fact, many tappers concentrate solely on the *sounds* of their dance; body movements hardly matter to them.

You've Got Rhythm

Anyone can learn to tap dance. Age, height, or weight make no difference in your ability to learn tap. You don't need a partner, and you don't always need musical accompaniment. As a tap dancer, you make your own music as you dance.

Once you've learned some steps, you can create your own routines and even invent new steps. And you'll be adding your own inspiration to a true American invention.

The Teach Yourself Tap Dancing Kit

Your kit includes:

1. **STICK-ON TAPS** that fit the soles and heels of your shoes. Before attaching your taps, read the instructions very carefully. Once on, these taps can't be removed.

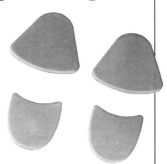

2. **TEACH YOURSELF TAP DANCING AUDIO TAPE.** Side One, *The Sounds of Tap*, lets you hear the different sounds of tap steps and rhythms described in this book. Side Two, *Tap Tunes*, contains short classic piano tunes to use for practicing or performing.

3. **THIS BOOK.** *Teach Yourself Tap Dancing* contains a short history of this great American invention, plus eight lessons that will teach you some basic steps, a fun routine, and lots of rhythms for improvising and creating your own dance.

AMERICA'S TRUE FOLK DANCE

● ●

Tap dancing was invented in America, beginning in Colonial times. African slaves, who had been brought to the New World to labor on the plantations of the southern colonies and the West Indies, learned new dances from their European masters. The slaves blended the steps of these dances with the body movements and rhythms of their own African dances. Over the years, new dance styles such as the Juba or the Ring Shout emerged.

Today's version of tap dancing came from the streets of New York City in the 1840s, where poor Irish immigrants and freed

Jimmy Doyle and Harland Dixon, 1912 – 1921, "the classiest two-man hoofing act in show biz."

African slaves were neighbors in the city's ghettos. To entertain themselves, they invented and exchanged dance steps, each group drawing upon its own heritage for inspiration. (An important contribution was the Irish jig, with its fast footwork, and the English clog dance, a noisy, foot-stomping dance done in wooden shoes.) The unique sound of clicking heels and toes against the ground became known as tap dancing.

Cakewalks and Struts

During the next 50 years (from about 1840 to 1890), the most popular form of theatrical entertainment in America was the minstrel show, which included comedy routines, singing, and dancing — all derived from America's black culture. Because blacks were not then permitted to perform on stage in theaters attended by whites, the white performers wore "black-

The Old Soft Shoe

In minstrel days, George Primrose was the master of Soft Shoe, an elegant and popular dance style done with tapless soft-soled shoes. Always beautifully dressed with hat, cane, and high collar, Primrose had the sophistication and grace of Fred Astaire and was the inspiration for many famous tappers. Many phrases you may have heard before were inspired by Primrose, since he was the first "Song and Dance Man," and his Soft Shoe became the centerpiece of many a "Class Act."

The Buck and Wing

At the turn of the century all tap dancing was called "buck and wing," and tappers were known as "buck dancers." To perform a wing, a dancer swung his leg out to the side while tapping. Different wing steps were called Pump, Pendulum, Saw, Fly, Rolling, Stumbling, and Double Back.

Tap great Baby Laurence demonstrates another way to get off the ground.

face" makeup to mimic black performers. One of the most popular minstrel acts was tap dancing. Over the years, touring minstrel troupes introduced this "new" dance to cities and towns all across America.

Fancy Footwork

By the early 1900s America had lost interest in minstrel shows. The new popular theater was the vaudeville show. Vaudeville was like today's talent shows, with singers, musicians, dancers, magicians, comics, acrobats, and other performers each presenting their act, one after the other. Over the next 35 years, tap dancing became one of America's favorite dancing styles in vaudeville — as well as in nightclub acts, Broadway shows, and in the movies.

During that time, tap dancing developed in different ways. Black dancers, often called "hoofers," created a tap dance style based on jazz syncopations (rhythms) with lots of improvisation. A hoofer primarily used his feet to tap out the dance rhythm and rarely moved his arms other than just swinging them at his sides. Many hoofers took great pride in their own unique tap styles and tricky dance routines and would criticize anyone who tried to copy them. Hoofers regularly challenged each other to "cutting contests," where teams of judges decided which one was the best tap dancer.

Glamorous Tap

Meanwhile, white tap dancers adopted a "show dance" style for Broadway shows and the movies. This style

The Time Step

Early in the century, tap dancers began to use a combination of shuffle, flap, and step as a way to tell the band how fast to play the music. The Time Step became as personal as a tapper's own name. King Rastus Brown, one of the great hoofers of the 1920s, developed the Time Step most dancers use today.

Broadway and Hollywood featured "precision" dancing, with rows of tapping chorus girls — or boys.

used comparatively simple rhythms in a highly polished dance routine with a lot of arm gestures, body movements, turns, leaps, and other dance steps. American musicals of the 1920s, 1930s, and early 1940s celebrated the tap dance with extravagant stage productions that featured many famous tap dancers and dance couples.

For the next twenty years, Hollywood and the American theater lost interest in tap dancing, and it was only kept alive in dance studios and dance schools. In the mid-1960s tap dancing once again became popular, this time as a nostalgia craze. Tap dancing is now recognized as an important part of America's cultural heritage. Today tap dancing is as popular as ever.

At Macy's annual Tap-O-Mania in New York City, thousands of tappers form a giant chorus line along Broadway.

STARS OF TAP DANCING

Bill "Bojangles" Robinson, 1878-1949

Bill Robinson was the most famous tapper of his time. Bojangles first appeared in the show *Blackbirds of 1928* doing his "lightning stair dance," and he became an overnight sensation. Robinson's dance style was considered neat with very clean footwork. He danced mostly on his toes with very few heel taps.

Bill "Bojangles" Robinson

John W. Bubbles

John W. Bubbles (John Sublett), 1902-1986

Half of the team of Buck and Bubbles, John W. Bubbles invented "rhythm tap" (a way of putting more taps into a musical phrase), and used his heels as well as his toes to make tap sounds at a time when tappers danced mostly up on their toes. The inspiration for many other tappers, John Bubbles is considered one of the all-time greats.

Charles "Honi" Coles (right)

Charles "Honi" Coles, 1911-

The team of Coles and Atkins (with Cholly Atkins) was considered the last of the great "class" acts, and Honi Coles performed a precise and elegant soft shoe. A disciple of John Bubbles, Honi Coles perfected high-speed rhythm taps, and in turn was the teacher of many of the young tappers of the 1970s and 80s.

Fred Astaire 1899-1987

Probably the best known and most widely admired dancer in America, Fred Astaire combined many kinds of dancing in his Hollywood movies, including tap . Astaire exuded grace and elegance in his top hat and tails, and never seemed to be working very hard, even when performing a difficult step. In some movies he created "trick" dances, such as dancing on the ceiling or dancing with a broom. With his frequent partner Ginger Rogers, Astaire inspired thousands of movie-goers to sign up for dance lessons.

Fred Astaire

Fayard and Harold Nicholas

Fayard and Harold Nicholas
1918-
1921-

The Nicholas Brothers became stars in 1932, when at the ages of fourteen and eight, they performed at Harlem's Cotton Club. Appearing in many movies of the 1930s and 40s, the Nicholas Brothers were one of the greatest "flash" acts — acrobatic performers and great dancers.

Eleanor Powell, 1912-1982

Of all the female dancers in Hollywood movies of the 1930s and 40s, Eleanor Powell was the best. She had a strong, energetic tap dancing style which shone through the elaborate staging and costumes of her movies. At a time when most women only followed their dance partners' lead, Powell performed many solos and duets with great skill. Fred Astaire once said "Elly put 'em down like a man"— he was talking about her feet — and he meant it as a compliment.

Eleanor Powell

Gregory Hines

Gregory Hines, 1946-

Born into a dancing family, Gregory Hines joined the act at age two. By five years old he was playing night-clubs (his act was called Hines Kids), and at eight he was on Broadway. His performance in *Eubie!* won him a Tony award nomination, and movies such as *Tap* and *White Nights* show off his individual, hard driving style.

Savion Glover, 1974-

Savion Glover is tap dancing's rising star. Raised in Newark, New Jersey, Savion began music lessons at age three, and tap lessons soon after. He made his movie debut when he was fifteen in the 1989 film *Tap*. By then he'd already starred on Broadway for two years in *The Tap Dance Kid*. Noted for his extremely fast footwork, Savion is considered by older professionals to be the leader of the next generation of tappers.

Savion Glover

START OFF ON THE RIGHT FOOT

. . . .

In the early days of tap dancing, dancers wore shoes with raised wooden soles, known as "clogs." Sometimes barefooted dancers would place bottle caps between their toes to make the tapping sound. Many people tap dance with just a pair of leather-soled and leather-heeled shoes. Today's tap shoes use metal plates attached to the toe and heel of each shoe, which makes a distinctive metal tapping sound.

Making Your Own Tap Shoes

Find a pair of your old, comfortable shoes. Be sure the toes are not curled up and the heels are not worn down on a slant. That would make it difficult to attach the taps. Check with a parent to make sure the shoes you've chosen are okay to use since it will be difficult to get the taps off once they are attached.

Attaching the Stick-On Taps

The stick-on taps in this kit will fit both right and left shoes of any size. The larger, triangular taps fit the toes, and the smaller, horseshoe-shaped taps fit the heels.

First, clean the sole and the heel surfaces of both shoes using a little soap and a damp cloth or paper towel. Then let them thoroughly dry. This cleaning step is very important because the taps will only stick well to a clean, dry surface.

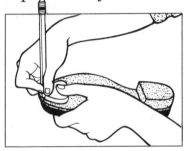

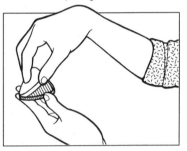

1. Rest one shoe upside down on your lap or on a tabletop. Center the taps side to side and line them up with the tips of the toes and the backs of the heels (see the diagram on the card in your kit). Using a pencil, trace the position of all four taps on the bottom of the shoes.

2. Remove the backing paper from one side of a toe-shaped adhesive piece. Carefully match the sticky side to the underside of a toe tap and press to attach.

WARNING

The edge of the taps may be sharp before the adhesive is attached. Handle the taps very carefully.

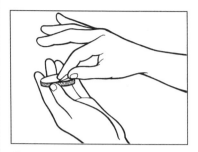

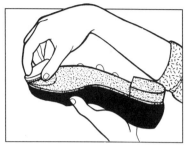

3. Remove the remaining piece of backing paper, trying not to touch the sticky surface.

4. Hold the tap with the sticky side slightly above the sole or heel of the shoe and position the tap exactly before pressing it firmly in place.

Repeat this process for the other three taps.

Position the taps very carefully. The adhesive will stick only once. After the taps are attached, they should not be removed. And the longer they stay attached, the stronger the adhesive bond will get.

If the stick-on taps must be removed or if they are accidently pulled off, they can be re-attached using a latex contact cement. Be sure to follow the manufacturer's directions.

Where to Practice

The more you practice tap dancing, the better you'll be. But you don't need to be wearing your tap shoes in order to practice, so you can practice anywhere — while waiting for a bus or an elevator, for example.

When you do practice with your tap shoes on, you can use almost any hard, smooth surface, but hardwood floors will give you the best sound. Be wary of dancing on waxed or highly polished wood floors, or on smooth tile floors — the slippery surface could be dangerous. Unpolished cement floors and sidewalks are okay, but will quickly wear down the taps.

If you have a hard time finding a place to practice, you might make a special practice floor. Try a 4-foot-square sheet of ½-inch-thick plywood, smooth side up. (You'll need help carrying it, though.) Ask the lumber yard for inexpensive plywood "cut offs." Masonite or particle board can also work well.

Wherever you practice, make sure your tapping and music won't bother anyone.

If your taps become nicked or rough from a cement surface, use fine sandpaper to file them smooth again.

Once the taps are attached and you've found the right place to practice,

Practice Tips

Do everything slowly at first and then gradually build up speed. Learn a step at a time by repeating it eight times on the right foot, then eight times on the left foot, counting steadily. Go on to four times right, four times left, then two and two, and one and one. This routine will also help you learn to switch from one foot to the other while still keeping time. And *always* bend your knees.

you're ready to begin learning to tap dance.

Concentrate on making your feet produce the right sounds on the right beats. Your ears will tell you how well you are doing. Always start a practice session with a warm-up routine.

Warm-Up Routine

Warming up loosens your body, helps you move more easily, and prevents strain. As you practice, try to keep your body relaxed and your knees bent.

1. Stand with your legs about shoulder-width apart. Slowly raise your arms over your head to the count of four. With arms raised, bend forward at the waist to touch your fingers to the floor. Bounce your fingers against the floor four times. Slowly straighten your body to its first position.

2. Raise your right leg straight out and shake it! Make your whole leg loose and floppy, like a rag doll's leg. Do the same with your left leg.

Using the Book and Tape Together

Side One of the audio tape lets you hear the sound of the tap steps and rhythms in the book.

The first time you try a lesson read the instructions in the lesson and try the step. Then listen to the same lesson on the tape while looking at the step pictured in the book. Then try it again on your own.

3. Raise your right foot and rotate it at the ankle, as if you were drawing a circle in the air with your big toe. Draw slowly, then draw fast. Change directions. Repeat with your left foot.

4. Run in place while you count to twenty. Then run in place on just the balls of your feet for another count of twenty.

You may have noticed as you ran in place that the sounds you made with your taps changed when you ran only on the balls of your feet instead of flat-footed. Each tap step has a unique sound. Listen for the different sounds on Side One of the audio tape and as you practice.

LESSON ONE: STAMP

1. Stand with your weight on your left foot, right foot forward.

2. Stamp your right foot so both the ball and heel of the foot hit the floor at the same time.

Alternate stamping your foot with clapping your hands (stamp/clap, stamp/clap). Do the same rhythm with your left foot. Try other combinations of stamp/clap, such as "stamp, stamp, clap, clap, stamp, stamp, stamp." Now try matching the rhythm of a song with your stamp/clap combinations. Practice the stamp with each foot.

Variation: The Step

Many routines call for a "step" instead of a "stamp". A "step" is made the same way as a stamp, but more gently, without force. You may do a step with your whole foot or only on the ball of your foot.

LESSON TWO: BALL CHANGE

● ●

The ball change is a basic tap step that shifts your weight from one foot to the other, giving a "tap, tap" sound.

1. Standing with your feet together and your knees slightly bent, raise your right foot and bring it slightly behind your left foot.

2. Put your right toe down with all the weight on the ball, making a "tap." At the same time as your make the tap, quickly lift your left foot.

To do a "ball change left" begin with the left foot. To do a "ball change right" begin with the right foot.

3. Land on the ball of your left foot and shift your weight to the left foot. Now repeat the step.

If you want to travel as you do this step, bring your left foot to the side for the second tap.

You can make the second tap with the whole foot instead of the ball of the foot. The sound will be different.

Try a ball change/clap combination to seven counts, with "stamp, stamp" on the eighth count (ball change/clap seven times, stamp right, stamp left).

By adding a stamp you can reverse your ball changes (ball change right, stamp right; ball change left, stamp left).

LESSON THREE: SHUFFLE

• •

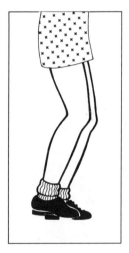

1. Start with your right foot raised and a bit behind.

2. Swing your foot forward, toe pointed down, so that your toe *brushes* the floor for a moment, making a sound.

3. Continue the swing a bit more forward and up.

The rhythm for the shuffle is "tap, tap, and pause." Try a shuffle/step: Shuffle the right foot, then step right, shifting your weight to the right foot. Now shuffle the left foot, and step left, shifting your weight to the left foot.

4. Now swing your foot back again, *brushing* the floor with your toe for another sound.

5. Bring your foot back to the starting position.

Try a shuffle/ball change: shuffle the right foot, ball change right (your weight will be on your left foot). Step on your right foot and do a shuffle/ball change beginning with the the left foot.

LESSON FOUR: THE WALTZ CLOG

· ·

Once you've got the three steps down, you're ready to combine them into a classic time step — the waltz clog. To do it, you repeat the three steps you just learned as follows: step, shuffle, ball change. The rhythm is 3/4 time, that is, "ONE, and two, and three; One, and two, and three."

1. Start with your right foot slightly raised ,your weight on your left foot.

2. Step in place, shifting your weight to your right foot.

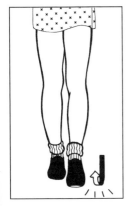 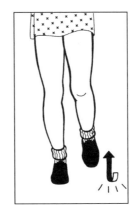

3. Then shuffle your left foot, and. . .

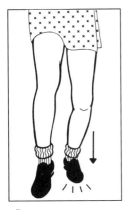 

4. ball change left (your weight is now on the right foot).

Repeat using the left foot (step left, shift your weight to your left foot, shuffle the right foot, ball change right, leaving your weight on the left foot ready to begin again with the right foot.)

A waltz clog variation is "step, brush, hop." Step to the right, brush forward with your left foot (that's the first half of a shuffle), then hop a bit on your right foot, keeping your left foot extended forward as you hop. Now repeat to the left.

Lesson Five: More Things to Do With Your Feet

Heel Drops

1. Stand on both feet with your right heel raised off the floor and both knees slightly bent.

2. Drop your right heel onto the floor, lifting the left heel at the same time.

3. Then lift up the right heel as you drop the left heel.

Alternate heel drops slowly at first, gradually getting faster. Make sure you can hear each heel tap clearly. Try out different rhythms entirely with heel drops.

Heel Digs

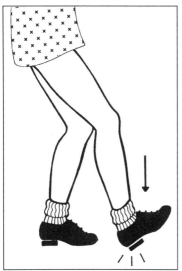

1. Dig the heel of one foot into the floor with your toes pointing upward.

Can you balance there? The dig makes a small tap sound of its own. Make a little step out of heel digs (right heel dig, right step; left heel dig, left step).

2. Dig in the heel of the other foot.

Tap Steps — It's All in the Name

Flap	Shuffle
Scuffle	Brush
Dig	Cramp roll
Hop	Stomp
Drop	Boogie
Click	Ball change
Scoot	Riff
Stamp	Slap
Chug	Pull back
Leap	Maxie Ford

Toe Punches

Lift your left foot slightly in back of you, toe pointing to the floor. Punch the tip of the toe into the floor and quickly pick it up again.

Try this step: stamp right, toe punch left, stamp left, toe punch right.

Hops

You already know how to hop. In tap dancing, you can vary your hops by making them loud and heavy or soft and light.

1. To make them loud, land on the whole foot.

2. To make them light, land only on the ball of the foot.

Hop in place, travel to the front, travel backward, turn while hopping.

Flaps

1. Place your feet side-by-side with your weight on the ball of the left foot. Bend your right knee slightly and pick up your right foot so it is a bit behind you.

2. Swing your right foot forward, toe pointed down, and "brush" the floor with your toe, making a sound. Continue slightly forward with your foot after you brush.

3. Then step on the ball of that foot, making a tap sound. Lift your left foot, so that you're ready to do a flap with that foot.

Try flaps alternating feet. You can stay in one place, or travel forward or backward as you step.

Heel and Toe Clicks

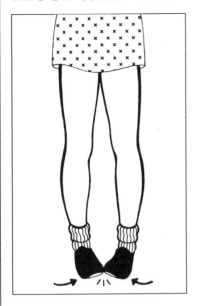

1. Standing on the balls of both feet with your heels about 2 inches apart, beat your heels together making a thud sound. (If your taps stick out on the sides of your shoes you'll get a metallic sound, but a thud is okay.)

2. For toe clicks, lean back on your heels and draw your little toes down while beating the toe edges of your shoes together.

Make a continuous step out of clicks: rock back on your heels, making a sound on the floor with both heels; click your toes; rock forward onto the balls of your feet making a sound with both toe taps; click your heels; rock back, click toes; rock forward, click heels. Now try two heel and toe clicks between rocks: rock, click, click; rock, click, click.

Cramp Rolls

The secret of good cramp rolls is to keep each tap clear and separate. Begin with the "lazy man's cramp."

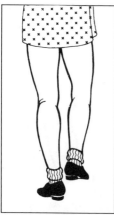

1. With your weight on your left foot pick up the right foot.

2. Then put it down toe first, then heel, making two taps. Raise the left heel off the floor as the right heel drops.

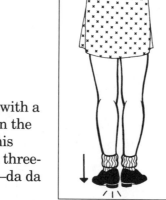

3. Follow with a heel drop on the left foot. This gives you a three-tap gallop—da da DUM.

Four Tap Cramp Roll

The rhythm for this is "da da da DUM." Make sure you can hear each tap clearly, like a drum roll, and see how fast you can roll them.

1. Begin with your weight on both feet.

2. Hop onto the ball of the right foot, making one tap.

3. Now put down the ball of the left foot, making the second tap.

4. Drop the right heel, making the third tap.

5. Then drop the left heel, making the fourth tap.

Chugs

1. Stand on the left foot, right foot slightly raised.

2. Pick up the left heel and. . .

3. scoot the left foot forward, shifting your weight forward and making a sliding sound. Then drop your heel.

You can chug both feet at the same time in a "double chug." A backwards-moving chug is called a "scoot back."

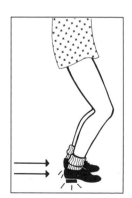

LESSON SIX: TURNS

• •

You can make up all sorts of turns out of the steps you've learned.

The X Turn

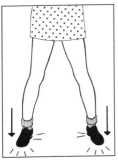

1. Jump forward with legs about shoulder-width apart.

2. Then jump with your legs crossed.

3. Turn on the balls of your feet and jump forward again.

4. You'll be facing backwards now; repeat once more and. . .

5. you'll face front again.

The O Turn

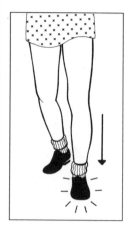

1. Stamp with your left foot.

2. Spin on the ball of your right foot,

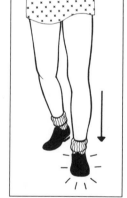

3. Stamp the left foot again as you come full circle.

You can chug, brush/step, step/hop, or almost any other combination of steps in circular motion, as long as it's all to the beat.

LESSON SEVEN: RHYTHMS

Rhythm is everything in tap dancing. Tappers often teach one another dance steps by reciting the rhythm in "scat," a jazz vocalization that sounds, for example, like "boo-de-lee-op bop she-bop." Tap rhythms can come from songs, rhymes, mechanical sounds (such as the old steam engine train step), or whatever you may hear in your own head. You can tap out a rhythm exactly, using one tap sound for each beat of the rhythm, or you can be more elaborate, adding taps to certain beats and leaving other beats silent.

Here are some familiar rhythms and corresponding steps you can try. Sing or hum the rhythm first. Try translating it into scat, even if you just say "dum de dum." Then try the steps while singing or scatting.

Rhythm Tricks

One way tappers remember a Time Step rhythm is by reciting the rhyme "**Thanks** for the bug**gy** ride (accents in boldface), with a tap for each syllable. To add an extra tap (for a Double Time Step), they'd say "**Thank** you for the bug**gy** ride." One more tap? Say "**When** will we **take** a bug**gy** ride." And for the ultimate Time Step, "**What**'ll I **do** with a bug**gy** ride?"

HICKORY DICKORY DOCK

Hick-o	ry	Dick-o	ry	Dock
right foot shuffle	**right foot step**	**left foot shuffle**	**left foot step**	**right stamp**

ROW, ROW, ROW YOUR BOAT

Row	Row	Row	Your	Boat
right stamp	**left stamp**	**right stamp**	**right chug**	**left stamp**

Repeat on the same side, hop instead of chug, or turn on the hop for a variation.

TRAIN STEP

Chug	Chug	Chug	Chug
right stamp in front of left	**left step back**	**right step back**	**left step forward**

The train starts slowly and gradually picks up speed. Repeat the steps, moving faster as the train leaves the station. Remember to blow the whistle — "Whoo-ooo!"

THE LONE RANGER THEME SONG (WILLIAM TELL OVERTURE)

Ba-de-dum	Ba-de-dum	Ba-de dum	Bum	Bum
3-count cramp roll	**3-count cramp roll**	**3-count cramp roll**	**right stamp**	**left stamp**

DRUM ROLL

Ba-da-de-dum   Ba-da-de-dum   Ba-da-de-dum
      (pause)   (pause)

4-count cramp roll	**4-count cramp roll**	**4-count cramp roll**

De-dum   De-dum
right-left heel drops   **right-left heel drops**

ONE POTATO, TWO POTATO

One	Po-ta	to	Two	Po-ta
right foot step	**left foot shuffle**	**left foot brush forward**	**left foot step**	**right foot shuffle**

to	Three	Po-ta	to	Four
right foot brush forward	**right foot step**	**left foot shuffle**	**left foot brush forward**	**left foot stamp**

SHAVE AND A HAIRCUT — TWO BITS

(an old vaudeville ending to a dance or joke)

Shave	and	a Hair	cut (pause)
jump forward on both feet	**pause**	**jump back right, then left**	**right step**

Two	Bits
left stamp	**right stamp**

RADIO TAP

Fred Astaire once described the sound of his tap dancing on radio as a "string of 'ricky ticky ticky tacky ticky tacky' steps." Just repeating that phrase out loud will tell you the rhythm of his dance! Here's at least one way to recreate Fred's radio style: Experiment to see if you can find others.

Ricky-ticky		Ticky-tacky		Ticky-tacky		Ticky-tacky	
left	**right**	**left**	**right**	**right**	**left**	**left**	**right**
heel-	**heel-**	**heel-**	**shuffle**	**heel-**	**shuffle**	**heel-**	**shuffle**
toe	**toe**	**toe**		**toe**		**toe**	

After you've tried each rhythm, see if you can make up a different combination of steps for it.

In *Singin' in the Rain*, Gene Kelly performs a Broadway musical-style number with a dancing chorus.

LESSON EIGHT: CREATING A DANCE

When you feel comfortable making up phrases for different rhythms, you're ready to combine phrases to make a dance — that is, to "choreograph" it.

You may want to emphasize either the rhythm of the music, the mood, or the dramatic meaning of a song's words. The emphasis you choose will affect your choreography.

Try "Hickory Dickory Dock" from Lesson Seven:

Hick-o	ry	Dick-o	ry	Dock
right foot shuffle	**right foot step**	**left foot shuffle**	**left foot step**	**right stamp**

If you practice the first line you'll notice that certain tap steps work best for accents or long beats, such as the stamp on the word "Dock." Other steps, such as the shuffle, make small sounds for short beats, as in "Hickory."

Now think about the next line of the verse. On the following page it is written with the "count" (one, two, three, etc.) and the accents (➡ = long or strong, ○ = short or weak):

1	**2,3**	**4**	**5,6**	**1**	**2**	**(3,4,5,6)**
The	mouse	ran	up	the	clock	(pause)

To tap only once for each beat, you might chug on the short accents and stamp on the long ones, accenting the stamp (chug **stamp**, pause, chug **stamp**, pause, chug **stamp**).

To tap more than once each beat, you could tap the line exactly as the first one, or with variations. Or, think about the words of the line and combine steps that show a running movement, as the "mouse ran up the clock."

The third and fourth lines have identical counts and accents:

1	**2,3**	**4**	**5,6**
The	clock	struck	one

1	**2,3**	**4**	**5,6**
The	mouse	ran	down

You might make a phrase going in one direction for the first of these two lines (forward, or to the right). Then, reverse direction for the second line (backward, or to the left).

The final line is the same as the first. When you put them all together, you have a dance.

Here is another familiar song, written out with time, with beats, and in phrases. How would you choreograph this song?

1	and 2	and	three	and a	four
All	around	the	mul	berry	bush

and	1	and	2	and	3 and	4
The	mon	key	chased	the	wea	sel

and	1	and	2	and	3	and	4
The	mon	key	thought	t'was	all	in	fun

1	and	2	and	3 and	4
Pop!		goes	the	wea	sel

Choreography Tips

★ Choose a short song or tune

★ To add drama, try adding taps during silent pauses, or breaks, in the music; try "freezing" — stopping and holding a pose for a beat or two — during the music

★ Balance your dance — most tunes repeat their phrases, usually at beginning and end; repeat a phrase or two of your dance.

★ Don't limit yourself to nursery rhymes. If you want to try longer tunes, here's a list of Beatles songs that always make great tap numbers:

When I'm 64
Yellow Submarine
Obla Di Obla Da
Paperback Writer
Hello Goodbye
Hole in My Head
In My Life
Lovely Rita Meter Maid

PUTTING ON A SHOW

· ·

Y ou've practiced your tap steps, tap music is humming in your head, and maybe you've already worked out a dance. Now it's time to create an act.

Your act can be a real performance that gives you a chance to "show your stuff" — and also gives your audience a good time.

Most acts are quite short. For a beginner, a minute or two will seem long enough. A tap act can be a complete production number that includes music, costume, props, and scenery. But even if your act has no scenery and only a top hat for a costume, it will have an opening, middle, and ending. You can develop a solo act by yourself, a partner act with a friend, or even a group act with other tap dancers.

Music

I f you haven't already chosen music or chore-ographed your dance, you

Flash or Class?

I f your act includes a lot of wild movements, acrobatics, tricky moves, or extremely fast foot-work, you've got a Flash Act. If your act is more elegant and refined, emphasizes precision, or is slower and romantic, you're a Class Act.

can use one of the tunes on Side Two of the audio tape. You can also choose one of the classic tap tunes listed here along with suggestions for staging your act. Most of the music can be borrowed from your public library. Any music or song you know can be the basis of a great tap act if it inspires you to dance and has a "toe-tapping" rhythm. Keep your ears open for great tap tunes, but avoid music with too heavy a drum beat or a loud percussion part — your feet will provide the percussion.

Famous Acts

★ Coles and Atkins
★ The Nicholas Brothers
★ Buck and Bubbles
★ Tip, Tap, and Toe
★ Chuck and Chuckles

Buck and Bubbles ("Buck" Washington and John W. Bubbles) had the same act for over twenty years — from the time Buck was six and Bubbles was ten.

Classic Tap Acts

Gene Kelly (here, with Debbie Reynolds) created a classic (and wet) act in *Singin' in the Rain*.

Singin' in the Rain

Costume Umbrella, raincoat, rain hat
Act Fun in the rain: splashing in puddles, playing, pouring water out of your hat

Take Me Out to the Ball Game

Costume Baseball hat and glove
Act Mimic the ball player's actions by pitching, swinging, and catching. You can also mimic the umpire.

Me and My Shadow

Costume The "shadow" tapper wears black
Act Two tappers perform in unison, one behind and to the side of the other.

Tea for Two

Costume Fancy party clothes
Act Dance around a small table and two chairs while pretending to pour tea.

East Side West Side

Costume   Jeans or shorts with cap and over size shirt

Act   Mimic jumping rope and playing hopscotch.

Tiptoe Through the Tulips

Costume   Loose, breezy, bright-colored clothing

Act   Dance around, in between, and over several flower pots with paper tulips.

There's No Business Like Show Business

Costume   Clown outfit and/or clown makeup

Act   Clown tricks and silliness; some tumbling and laughing.

Alexander's Ragtime Band

Costume   Band uniform

Act   A marching band: drum major, trumpeter, piccolo player, big bass drum.

The West Point Story featured James Cagney and a lot of military-style dancing.

Your Entrance

Most of your act will be your dance routine, but it may have a special entrance as well. Here are a few possibilities.

THE SILENT ENTRANCE: Walk out in silence, take your place, and begin dancing when the music starts. Another version is to dance out in silence (perhaps a left-right shuffle walk), strike a pose, then begin your dance when the music starts.

THE MUSICAL ENTRANCE: Some tunes have an introduction or lead-in before the main melody. You can start the music while you are still off-stage, then dance out to your place during the introduction and start your main dance routine when the melody begins.

CREATE AN ENTRANCE: Maybe you can whistle yourself onstage or clap the rhythm with your hands. With the help of a friend, you might dance onstage to a drum beat or some other percussion instrument, or to the sound effects of bird songs, ocean waves, hammering or sawing, something humorous, or whatever sound fits the mood of your dance.

Your Exit

A good act always has a good finish, whether it's a daredevil split or a quiet fade-out. You might just finish your act onstage and exit during the applause, or make the exit a part of your dance routine. Whatever you choose to do, make sure it suits the mood of your dance — elegant and refined, flashy, or funny.

OFF TO BUFFALO: A classic vaudeville exit is called "Shuffle off to Buffalo." Here's how to do it:

  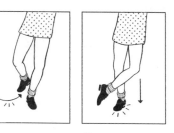

1. Hop to the left on your left foot.

2. Shuffle with your right foot.

3. Cross your right foot behind your left foot and step with your right foot.

Repeat until you're offstage.

THE SILENT EXIT: When the music ends, strike a pose. Hold it for a few seconds, take your bow, then walk or run offstage.

THE MUSICAL EXIT: Continue or repeat your dance while moving offstage as the music fades out. Then come back out to take your bow.

Dressing the Part

The music and theme you select will probably suggest the right costume for your act. Tap dance costumes do not have to be elaborate. You might only need the right shirt or hat to help project your theme.

Make sure your costume is comfortable and allows plenty of freedom of movement. Your costume should also be durable — you don't want it to rip or fall apart during a performance.

Be sure to practice your act while wearing your costume to make sure there are no hidden problems. You don't want to be tripping over pants that are too long, popping seams that are too tight, or trying to keep a hat that is too small on your head.

Props

Fred Astaire danced with mops, firecrackers, and a kitchen chair. Bill Robinson became famous for dancing up and down a flight of stairs!

Props are a great way to enhance your act. Some typical tap dance props include a top hat or straw hat and cane, an umbrella, a baton, feather boas, sports equipment, and a small flag.

Avoid using a prop that is heavy or breakable, or anything that could be dangerous and hurt you during a performance. This is tap dancing, not sword swallowing!

Performance Tips

1. Practice, practice, practice! Make sure your music, dance, entrance, and exit all go together, and that your costume and props work right.

2. Smile, smile, smile! Let your audience see you are enjoying yourself.

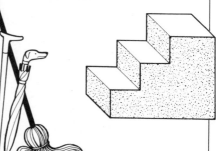

Partners

Invite a friend to join your act. Some classic tap acts, like Me and My Shadow or Tea for Two, are best as duets. Even if one of you is a more accomplished tapper than the other, you can have fun creating an act together. Try one of these duets:

SHADOWING: One dancer repeats everything the first dancer does, just after the first dancer does it. Vary the act halfway through by switching roles as lead dancer and shadow.

UNISON DANCING: Both dancers do exactly the same thing at the same time as perfectly together as possible.

STORYTELLING: Act out a story as you dance with your partner (keeping time with the music, of course). Use gestures and facial expressions to help tell your story.

Ginger Rogers was Fred Astaire's most popular dancing partner — here, in *Swingtime*.

MORE TAP!

Taking Tap Lessons

After you've learned the steps in this book, you may want to go on and take lessons from a tap dancing teacher. Tap dancing is traditionally passed on from teacher to student. Younger dancers learned from older ones through teaching and sharing tap steps, even if the teaching was out on the sidewalk instead of in a dance studio.

Look for a class with students your own age and a teacher who seems friendly. If you know

Savion Glover shows the other dance students his stuff in *Tap*.

someone who is already in a tap dance class, ask if the teacher will let you attend a class just to observe. Don't feel shy about asking a teacher about his or her dancing background, and if you'll be able to see the teacher in a tap performance. And be sure to ask if this class will give you a chance to perform too!

Attending tap performances — even student performances — can lead you to a tap teacher. After a performance, tap dancers usually like to talk to kids interested in tap. One of the dancers might be a teacher as well. Keep your eyes open for notices of tap performances in your community.

You can always look for tap dance classes in your local Yellow Pages under Dance Studios, or in the classified section of your newspaper. Your library may carry *Dance* magazine, which lists hundreds of dance schools and teachers by state.

Buying Tap Shoes

Although many tap shoes for children come with taps already attached, in most cases tap shoes and taps come separately. Many tap dancers just use a comfortable pair of shoes they already have. Tap shoes should be well fitting, even a bit snug, with sturdy leather soles and heels. They should have laces or straps to hold them on well. Loafers, sneakers, and shoes with very high heels don't work well.

Dance catalogs and dancewear stores offer a

variety of styles and colors of tap shoes. Some look just like regular street shoes while others are "character shoes" with bow ties, fancy straps and ribbons, and other decorations to complement a dance costume. All tap dance shoes have leather soles and heels.

Taps are usually installed by a shoe repair shop. The store where the taps are purchased will select the right size and shape of taps to fit your shoes. If you take tap lessons, your instructor will recommend a particular type of tap. In any case, aluminum taps attached with screws are better than taps made of another metal attached with nails.

When you pick up your tap shoes from the shoe repair shop, try them on before you leave. Be sure that the screws used to attach the taps do not stick out through the inside of the shoe. If the screws even make little bumps on the inside sole, there is a good chance they will eventually poke through and become very uncomfortable.

See that the bottom of the taps are smooth, and won't scratch the floor. Most important of all, make sure the edges of the taps do not stick out from the sole or heel of the shoe, which could make you trip.

Mail-Order Suppliers of Tap Dance Shoes, Taps, and Dance Accessories

Capezio Ballet Makers, Inc.
One Campus Road
Totowa, NJ 07512
(201) 595-9000

The Dance Shop
2485 Forest Park Boulevard
Fort Worth, TX 76110
(817) 923-0017

Kling's Theatrical Shoe Company
218 S. Wabash Avenue
Chicago, IL 60604
(312) 427-2028

Leo's Dancewear
1900 N. Narragansett
Chicago, IL 60639
(312) 889-7700

Taffy's by Mail
701 Beta Drive
Cleveland, OH 44143
(216) 461-3360

Stores That Sell Tap Dance Shoes, Taps, and Dance Accessories

Baum's
106-112 S. 11th Street
Philadelphia, PA 19107
(215) 923-2244

Capezio Dance Theater Shop
650 Broadway on 51st
New York, NY 10019
(212) 245-2130

Lebo's Inc.
4118 E. Independence Boulevard
Charlotte, NC 28205
(704) 535-5000

Leo's Dancewear
1900 N. Narragansett
Chicago, IL 60639
(312) 889-7700

Loshin's Dancewear
260 W. Mitchell Avenue
Cincinnati, OH 45232
(513) 541-5400

Miquelitos Dancing Shoes and Supplies, Inc.
7315 San Pedro Avenue
San Antonio, TX 78216
(512) 349-2573

Motion Unlimited
218 S. Wabash Avenue
Chicago, IL 60604
(312) 922-3330

Tap on Videotape

Hollywood movies from the 1930s and 40s were filled with wonderful tap dancing numbers. Although some of the movies themselves may be less than great, they give you a chance to see some of the stars of tap dancing in action. And thanks to videotape, you can just "fast-forward" from one great tap act to the next. Below are some interesting movies available on videotape. An asterisk (∗) next to a title means "highly recommended."

An American in Paris
1951, 115 minutes, not rated
Dancers: Gene Kelly, Leslie Caron

Anchors Aweigh
1945, 140 minutes, not rated
Dancers: Gene Kelly, Frank Sinatra

The Band Wagon
1953, 112 minutes, not rated
Dancers: Fred Astaire, Cyd Charisse

∗**Broadway Melody of 1940**
1940, 102 minutes, not rated
Dancers: Fred Astaire, Eleanor Powell, George Murphy

Dames
1934, 90 minutes, not rated
Dancers: Joan Blondell, Dick Powell, Ruby Keeler

Gene Kelly dances with cartoon character Jerry the Mouse in *Anchors Aweigh.*

Easter Parade
1948, 104 minutes, not rated
Dancers: Judy Garland, Fred
Astaire, Peter Lawford

Eubie!
1981, 85 minutes, not rated
Dancers: Gregory Hines, Terri
Burell, Maurice Hines

Flying Down to Rio
1933, 89 minutes, not rated
Dancers: Dolores Del Rio, Ginger
Rogers, Fred Astaire

Follow the Fleet
1936, 110 minutes, not rated
Dancers: Fred Astaire, Ginger
Rogers

Footlight Parade
1933, 100 minutes, not rated
Dancers: James Cagney, Ruby
Keeler, Joan Blondell, Dick
Powell

For Me and My Gal
1942, 104 minutes, not rated
Dancers: Judy Garland, Gene
Kelly, George Murphy

42nd Street
1933, 98 minutes, not rated
Dancers: Dick Powell, Ruby
Keeler, Ginger Rogers

Girl Crazy
1943, 99 minutes, not rated
Dancers: Mickey Rooney, Judy
Garland, June Allyson

The Great Ziegfeld
1936, 176 minutes, not rated
Dancers: William Powell, Myrna
Loy

**James Cagney dances with
Ruby Keeler in *Footlight
Parade*.**

Tap Music

Records and tapes of music
especially for tap dancing
are available from Hoctor
Records. Write or call for their
catalog and the name of a store
near you that sells their record-
ings.

Hoctor Records
157-159 Franklin Turnpike
Waldwick, New Jersey 07463
(201) 652-7767

Holiday Inn
1942, 101 minutes, not rated
Dancers: Bing Crosby, Fred
Astaire

Invitation to the Dance
1957, 93 minutes, not rated
Dancer: Gene Kelly

*** The Little Colonel**
1935, 80 minutes, not rated
Dancers: Shirley Temple, Lionel
Barrymore, Bill Robinson

Little Miss Broadway
1938, 70 minutes, not rated
Dancers: Shirley Temple, George
Murphy

*** The Littlest Rebel**
1935, 70 minutes, not rated
Dancers: Shirley Temple, Bill
Robinson

Ziegfeld Follies is the only
movie in which Fred Astaire
and Gene Kelly dance together.

The Pirate
1948, 102 minutes, not rated
Dancers: Judy Garland, Gene
Kelly, The Nicholas Brothers

Poor Little Rich Girl
1936, 72 minutes, not rated
Dancer: Shirley Temple

Rebecca of Sunnybrook Farm
1938, 80 minutes, not rated
Dancer: Shirley Temple

Shall We Dance?
1937, 109 minutes, not rated
Dancers: Fred Astaire, Ginger
Rogers

*** Singin' in the Rain**
1952, 102 minutes, not rated
Dancers: Gene Kelly, Debbie
Reynolds, Donald O'Connor

Bill "Bojangles" Robinson
dances with 6-year-old
Shirley Temple in *The
Littlest Rebel*.

*Swing Time
1936, 105 minutes, not rated
Dancers: Ginger Rogers, Fred
Astaire

*Tap
1989, 111 minutes, PG-13 for
profanity and violence
Dancers: Gregory Hines, Sammy
Davis, Jr., Harold Nicholas,
Bunny Briggs, Sandman Sims,
Steve Condos, Pat Rico, Arthur
Duncan, Savion Glover

*That's Dancin'
1985, 105 minutes, G
Dancers: Mikhail Baryshnikov,
Ray Bolger, Sammy Davis, Jr.,
Gene Kelly, Liza Minelli, others

That's Entertainment
1974, 135 minutes, G
Dancers: Judy Garland, Fred
Astaire, Frank Sinatra, Gene
Kelly, others

That's Entertainment Part II
1976, 132 minutes, G
Dancers: Gene Kelly, Fred
Astaire, others

**Greg Hines impresses a group of famous old-timers — Arthur
Duncan, Pat Rico, Harold Nicholas, Steve Condos, Sandman
Sims, Henry LeTang, and Sammy Davis, Jr. — in *Tap*.**

Fred Astaire leads a lineup of classy gents in *Top Hat*, the most stylish of 1930s dance movies.

Top Hat
* 1935, 99 minutes, not rated
Dancers: Fred Astaire, Ginger Rogers

Yankee Doodle Dandy
* 1942, 126 minutes, not rated
Dancers: James Cagney, Joan Leslie

Ziegfeld Follies
1946, 110 minutes, not rated
Dancers: Fred Astaire, Lucille Ball, William Powell, Judy Garland, Cyd Charisse, Gene Kelly